UNTRADITIONAL

A Collection of Passion-Fy Short Stories

by

DNC

UNTRADITIONAL

A Collection of Passion-Fy Short Stories

Copyright © 2015 by D. Coleman

Manufactured in the United States

ISBN-13: 978-0692569573 (Custom)

ISBN-10: 069256957X

Edited by: Dana Barka (Barka Communications)
             Jessica Williams (Williams Consultants)
             Elizabeth Drake-Boyt (Erete's Bloom)
Cover Design by: D. Coleman
Photo Taken by: Najla Slowe

This book is dedicated to the shy girls who may be scared to show the world their untraditional side.

Be fearless and go for your passion.

ACKNOWLEDGEMENTS

First, I want to thank my heavenly Father for allowing me to step out in this direction with the comfort of knowing it is the right step.

I want to thank my mom, Alfredda Allen, who taught me the value of going after what I want. You're not here physically, but I know that you have watched and guided me throughout this whole process. I've learned so much from your plight and I promise you that I will give my dream my all.

Next, I want to thank my family; my husband for always backing me on my passion and pushing me to do the things that make me happy NOW rather than later. I want to thank my kids for loving mommy unconditionally. I love you all more than words could ever describe. You guys are my hearts and I live for you.

I want to thank all my family, bonded by blood and not, who have supported me on this journey and even sometimes playing my muses. Your continuous love, pep talks and push to finally let this moment out was more than I could ever ask for.

I also want to thank my editors, content testers and just those who gave me advice on how to finally get this out. Your words and guidance will remain engraved in my writings present and future.

Last, I want to thank my readers. As the first of many books, I hope you remember this piece as much as I will remember that you took a chance on a new author. Thank you so much for stepping into my world of passion.   Have fun!

UNTRADITIONAL:

When you allow your desires to live beyond the constraints of a conventional world.

Passion-Fy: A genre of fiction dealing with intense emotion based upon untraditional sexual scenarios.
~DNC

TABLE OF CONTENTS

DREAMER

Just the thought of you,

Touching, teasing, pleasing me,

Is like a dream.

It's incredible what you could do,

If I just let you out of my dream.

But, would it be too much,

Knowing what you could do inside of me?

But, maybe this dream deserves to be our reality.

DAYDREAMING

THE ALARM WAS BLARING and I noticed it was 8:45am; fifteen minutes until my final psychology exam.

"Shit!"

I jumped up and threw on my sneakers. I ran into the bathroom to brush my teeth and my hair. I peeked in the mirror before I came out. *I look a mess*, I thought to myself, but I had to go. I was lucky to get out the apartment by 8:52am with less than ten minutes left before my exam. Good thing I was only five minutes from campus. I sped down side streets and grabbed a parking spot right in front of the McClure A&S building.

As I walked in the auditorium, I noticed that almost every seat was filled. I raced up the stairs knowing I only had seconds to get set to take the last test of my college life.

"Ava!"

I looked up into the fifth row from the top and saw Dominic. I was so happy to see he saved me a seat. As I finally got to my seat, Professor Sawyer stepped into the room.

"Man, could you cut it any closer?" Dominic questioned me.

I just laughed and thanked him.

"Alright class. Let's get it poppin'," Professor started on his semi-cool, but still very geekish rant before handing out the tests.

I was so happy that Dominic thought about me. Sure, I wanted to take my test, but I was more excited to take it next to him. Dominic was also a senior majoring in psychology, but not your normal psychology geek. He was 6'2", a solid 205 with sun-glazed skin and grey eyes. His voice was as deep and calming as a late-night, quiet storm deejay. Everything about him oozed player — an obvious hoe magnet — but I had never seen him treat any woman with disrespect. Not even with the hoes who threw themselves at him. I couldn't lie. I had a huge crush on him. The professor's rant made me fall into a normal Dominic daydream:

I saw the classroom empty and instead of Dominic sitting next to me, he was standing at the front of the room by the teacher's desk. I looked around and realized that we were truly alone.

"Come here," he called to me.

Without hesitation, I stood up and started walking down the stairs. I noticed that the shabby sweatpants and t-shirt I originally had on was now a black dress with two slits on the side, set off with some red four-and-a-half inch peep-toe stilettos.

I could even feel my hair blowing in some sort of hidden wind from within the classroom.

That's weird. I finally made it down the stairs and as I took that last step he used all his strength to knock everything off the desk. I knew what was next.

He gestured for me to give him my hand and I did. He pulled me in close and matched up our lips perfectly. His tongue was smooth and perfect. It knew exactly what it was doing. He pulled me closer by my ass and proceeded to lay me across the desk.

I lay back awaiting his next move. He got down on his knees and took his time taking my shoe off, kissing each toe and then moving his way up my calf. His hands led the way. He rubbed my thighs and then his mouth made it to the same location, not missing a spot. He rubbed my inner thighs and again kissed both without missing a spot. I let out a small groan and felt his hand move to my cove.

"Ava..." Dominic said.

"Yeah?" I whispered as I awaited his next move.

"Are you going to pass these down?"

"Huh?"

I was suddenly pulled from my fabulous dream and brought back to the present day downer, formally known as my classroom.

"Ah, the tests...yes, I will pass them down."

He laughed. He knew I daydreamed a lot, but he had no clue that he was the star of most of my mental screenplays. At least, I didn't think he did. . .

After we finished the test, we headed to the nearby bar to celebrate our last collegiate achievement. It was packed. I walked through the door to only get pushed back by some guy butting me in line.

"Hey Man, don't bump her."

Dominic's protection over me was so refreshing, seeing that I'd never had a guy friend who ever went that extra mile just to make sure I was ok.

I smiled at him. "Thanks!"

Dominic grabbed my hand and led me and a couple other classmates into the bar. I suddenly fell back into another dream as we all began ordering our meal:

The bar was full and roaring from excitement from the closure of finals week. We all sat at a table together with Dominic sitting right next to me. We told jokes, laughed and drank. Before I knew it, I was tipsy. Our classmate was in mid-conversation when I leaned over to Dominic and whispered, "I want you."

His face wasn't shocked, but excited, and he whispered back, "I want you, too."

I smiled and put my hand on his leg. He complemented my hand with his. First patting it and then moving it upward on his thigh. I could feel my blood pumping faster in that hand, anticipating what treasure I was going to find. Our hands moved higher and I began to feel the tip of his shaft...

"Hey, what do you want to drink?"

Damn it! It happened again. The real world once again hit me like a brick. I was totally confused by my own wild and tricky mind. Why was it so hard to stay in reality? It was like no matter what I did, or where I was, I couldn't stop thinking of him. I just wanted all of him, all the time.

Even with the disappointment of my daydream shattering, we still told jokes, laughed and drank. Before we knew it, the bar security starting escorting people out – one drunkard at time.

"Last call," the bartender told us. "Do you want something else?"

"No. I'm good." I told him. "Thanks for asking, though."

"Of course. I got your check." Dominic grabbed for my receipt.

"No, I have it," I grabbed it back out of his hand.

"No, for real. Let me take care of it one last time," he pleaded.

Like I said, Dominic was a gentleman and he loved taking care of me, so he handled most of the bills on our outings.

"Ok. I'm not going to fight you" I replied. *But if we were naked on the beach I would,* I thought to myself.

"I have a few leftovers from my graduation party. You want to come by for a few drinks?"

"Why not? Finals are OVER!" I screamed which made the bar explode in yells and chants. We laughed and headed out.

Dominic drove a 2014 Infiniti Hybrid. Yep, he was gorgeous *and* environmentally-conscious. I left my car on campus and rode back with him to his place.

When we first met, I tried my best to figure out how a young man from Miami, Florida had all this loot.

Based on his nerdy and gentle personality, I assumed he wasn't a drug dealer, but I did wonder if he was into something else – maybe prostitution. But after years of unsuccessful investigations, I just chopped up his wealth to an inheritance he received after his parents passed when he was only twelve.

We pulled up to his condo — yes condo in college — and took the elevator to the 12th floor. His apartment was definitely a bachelor's pad complete with full arcade games like Pacman and Duck Hunter and even a Baywatch pinball table. When you walked into his bar area, his walls were covered with Scarface posters and above his cabinets was a personal mini-liquor store. The ironic thing was that he wasn't a real drinker; just a social one.

"Let's see…You want Patron with a splash of sour mix?"

"How did you know?" I sarcastically answered.

It was an inside joke. He knew exactly what I loved, especially since he saw that same drink make its debut in our sophomore year, when I was just getting my drinking legs under me. That night at the bar, the drink's superpower took over and put me on my ass after just two glasses.

"I can't believe we're finally done. What are you going to do now?" I asked him.

"I don't know," he answered. "Don't judge me, but I might go to grad school."

"Really!?"

I never thought of Dominic as the bookworm. Yeah, he was a little nerdish in a gentle genius kind of way, but I figured with those brains and his looks, he could easily get a great job right out of school.

"What about you?" he bounced back to me.

"I don't know, either. Probably go find a good job and hope it's the one I want to retire at."

"I hear you." As he was answering, he leaned over and grabbed a picture frame next to his couch.

"Remember when we went to Jamaica for Spring Break?"

I moved closer to him and snatched the picture out of his hand.

"Of course I remember that trip. Sophomore year, right after we met. I thought you were gorgeous…"

I stopped my statement immediately, realizing the word-vomit that just came out of my mouth. I said just a little too much. . .

"Oh, really; I'm gorgeous, huh?"

We laughed and I nodded. And I tried to change the topic.

"Do you remember when you fell. . ." I started.

He interrupted me. "So why haven't you told me this before?"

A grin slowly grew on his face with his eyes now scanning my body for a response; as if he was waiting for something more telling than my words. It was intense, so I took a sip and allowed my word-vomit to continue.

"Honestly, I was hoping to keep it to myself. You're a great friend and I would never do anything to mess that up, you know."

He turned his body toward me on the couch, seemingly very interested in this new "gorgeous" topic.

"Why would you telling me that ever mess up our friendship?"

"I don't know, man. You've seen the movies." We both laughed.

I couldn't believe it. I was finally opening up my vault to reveal my most valuable secret. It felt amazing to let it go, but now I wondered about his feelings. Then we both went silent. Not an awkward silence, but more of a "what now?" silence.

He finally broke it. "I think you're kind of cute, too."

"Kind of!" I yelled back and jumped on him, wrestling him to the floor. We wrestled a lot and I enjoyed it each time. It gave me another reason to fantasize about him. Just feeling him touch me was so amazing, even if it was in a childish way.

I was winning the match when he chimed in.

"Hey, hey!" he yelled.

I slowed my attack on his body to listen.

"I think you should have said something before. I think...we could have been doing this before if you did...but maybe without any clothes on."

I was totally taken aback from his comment. I got off of him and sat on the couch. He sat up from the floor.

"Maybe that came out wrong," he added.

"It came out as if you would prefer to do something more than wrestle. Am I correct?"

I felt like my question was rhetorical. This was the first time anything like this had been brought up between us. I normally made sure to lock away my thoughts and feelings; my attraction and lust for him. But in that moment, I think we both knew the answer to my question.

He confirmed my assumption by standing up in front of me. I joined him. I wanted his lips more than I had ever dreamt before. So, this time I went for it.

I pulled his collar down, ensuring that my aim was on point. And for the first time ever I wasn't dreaming about this moment. I was living the moment.

I pressed my lips on his, slowing taking in our first kiss. His lips soon relaxed into mine and I felt his tongue meet mine for the first time; another first. The warmth of our mouths was enough to make my body melt. And then the kiss stopped. He turned toward his room and grabbed my hand, but did not take a step.

He turned back toward me, waiting for my command — after all, he was a true gentleman. I looked deep into those grey eyes of his and saw what I wanted. I nodded 'yes' to him and we walked back to his room.

I sat down on his bed as he closed the door.

"Before anything happens, I need to know," he started in "…what it is that you want?"

I arched my brow at him.

He sat down with me and restated his question.

"What do you want from this moment?"

"I want you out of my dreams"

He quietly laughed. "What dreams?"

"My daydreams."

"I don't think this is going to help," he responded.

"But it will." I answered back. "There will be no dreaming after this; just memories of my new reality."

I was now ready to get what I wanted.

"Now lie down" I told him.

I assumed he was a little in shock with my answer since he had never heard me talk in such a bold manner. So, I helped him by pushing him down and then falling on top of him. I kissed the top of his ear, slowly, and then licked around the edge. The room was so quiet that we both could hear our hearts racing.

I moved to his neck and took my time kissing from left to right and back left again.

He let out a little groan and I smiled through the kisses. He took his massive hands and began caressing my back and soon lowered them to my hips.

I put my hands on his abs and felt his six pack — chiseled and heating up from our pending contact.

"Are you ready?" He whispered in my ear.
I straddled him and sat straight up so he could see my response.

"Yes!" I exhaled.

I closed my eyes and allowed my dream to come to life.

LIKE A DRUG

In case you didn't know,

My pussy is like a drug.

Stronger than crack,

Smoother than ecstasy.

You can't import this,

This is addiction on first-hit shit.

In its purest form it can be deadly,

Trapping you in its toxic grip.

Making you forget your daily responsibilities,

Some straight junky "I need more" shit.

My pussy is like a drug

I would stray far away.

There's no telling what the power of this "P" would do to you,

So, do you dare take a taste?

THE PLEASURE PRINCIPLE:

Part I

IT'S HARD TO EXPLAIN my life. I get what I want, because I give what is wanted. From a young age, I found it easy to get attention from men – especially unintentional attention.

I fought many fights standing up for my essences especially in school. Girls were jealous because of who I am and how easily — and quickly — boys were attracted to me. But, never once did I intentionally lure any member of the male species into my world by dressing or acting a certain way — they were just very interested in me.

Maybe it's the sparkle in my eye, or the wave in my hair. Or, perhaps in the words of the great Maya Angelou, "It's the curl of my hips…and the roundness of my lips." Or, maybe the roundness of my ass, or the plumpness of my chest. Hell, it could be the whisper of my voice; I have no real clue other than I just seem to have great genes. No matter how undesirable I try to make myself, I still catch their attention. Even on my worst day, they can feel the charge of my presence entering the room.

This alluring essence, I carry inside, feels like a double-edged sword — for all the attention it got me that I wanted, it doubly gave me attention I didn't want.

Some call me "poison ivy" but my only poison is pleasure. I can't help it, but I absolutely enjoy giving pleasure; whether it's in a conversation with a complete stranger or an astounding eruption in the bedroom. I live for pleasure; my own and others.

But, I didn't realize that I would one day taste my own poison.

It was back when I first moved into my own apartment right after college. I was so excited to finally have my own place; my own furniture, my own food and my own rules. I decided to throw a housewarming party the Saturday after I finished unpacking, so I started a list and headed to the grocery store first.

I walked into the neighborhood McMike's Grocery to pick up drinks and snacks. Dressed in my relaxed, hood-chic outfit with loose grey sweatpants, a white wife-beater and my Yankee's hat, I entered the produce section. I was gliding toward the tomatoes in search of the ripest specimen, when a tantalizing, chocolate-skinned champion caught my eye. I knew as soon as we locked eyes that the "poison" was starting to make its way to him.

If he stepped one foot closer, it would be over for him. And so, he took that step.

I immediately felt bad for him. I glanced down to the floor, trying my best to guide him from my clutches, but it was too late.

Almost as if magnetized to each other, we met in front of the tomatoes. I could feel his eyes blazing through my clothes, dying to see what was hiding underneath. I did my best to ignore his presence, but his scent was exotic and soothing.

My urges were beginning to grow.

I quickly reached for a ripe tomato at the top of the stack. As I touched the tomato I felt his arm graze my chest, reaching under me for a lower tomato. As innocent as his movement was, I knew that it was a direct message to my body.

"Excuse me," we both chimed.

I turned to look at his face; his white, shining smile and deep brown eyes flicked with amber: a complement to God's work. Even his lips were juicy enough to bite. I turned from him again and proceeded to put the veggie in my arm basket.

"It's ok." I reassured him.

I turned and walked away as quickly as I could, trying again to release him from my trap. I even slowed my walk, hoping he wouldn't notice my wide hips and finely-tuned ass. My attempts to save him from my web were strong, but his efforts were stronger.

I continued my walk through the store stopping in the pasta aisle, then the juice aisle, then the liquor aisle. I don't know if it was by chance or strategic planning on his end, but we just so happened to end up meeting down the same aisles.

I passed another short, fair-skinned man on the way to the check-out counter.

"Hey, Beautiful!" he threw at me as I swiftly passed him.

I smiled because I didn't want to be rude, but became frustrated that I couldn't do something as simple as shopping without unwanted attention. I rushed to the shortest line. As I waited for the three people ahead of me, I heard the same "Excuse me" that had so gently grazed me in produce.

I turned to see my chocolate champion standing behind me.

"I really want to apologize about that incident earlier. I hope I didn't offend you," he said.

"No. It's ok. I know it was an accident," I answered knowing perfectly well it wasn't.

"My name is Mason...Mason Alexander." He held out his hand.

Dare I touch it? I guess if he is asking for it, I must please.

"My name is Taylor."

I took a step closer to the register. Two more people to go. *Can he be saved?*

"I know this is a little awkward," he persisted, "but I think you are gorgeous and would love to take you out. Will you allow me to do so? It would be a pleasure to learn more about you."

Pleasure. . .how could I not?

I obliged his request and gave him my number. Even though I knew the outcome was going to leave him breathless and addicted, at least he would enjoy it. I finally made it to the register and he assisted me by placing my groceries on the belt. He was kind and did what he needed to get my attention. He pleased me, and this intrigued me to see more. I waved good-bye to him as I walked out the door.

As I crossed the street, a blacked-out Range Rover parked next to my car caught my attention. Women from across the street took their time slowly walking into the store, biding their time, waiting for the driver to exit. A six-four, fair-skinned stallion stepped out of the driver's side and his much shorter, less-attractive friend jumped out the passenger side.

Again, I did my best not to look directly at him. I rushed past him only to have him stop and stare me down as I moved to my trunk.

I popped the trunk and immediately heard his door close and some steps get closer and louder.

"Thank you," A raspy voice spoke to me, much deeper than I expected.

I stopped to think about what he'd said exactly.

Thank you for what?

I looked over my trunk to see this light, clear-complexioned man with a perfectly lined reddish-brown goatee looking down at me.

"I'm sorry. Did you say 'thank you'?" I asked.

"Yes, thank you."

I rolled my eyes and sent a small chuckle into the air.

"Thank you for what?"

I couldn't wait to hear what type of line this was. I was sure I'd heard it a million times. The intro may be a little different, but the hook was always the same.

"Thank you for passing me. I was having a rough day, but then I noticed you and you changed that — so thank you."

He took a step closer and I turned toward him taking in all of his greatness.

"Thank you, Beautiful. It was a pleasure." He grabbed my hand and gave it a soft kiss. Then he turned to meet up with his friend who was waiting for him outside the store.

Normally, a man would go for the digits, but he didn't even ask. And I was actually ready to give them.

How dare he!?

Or, was he just really smart and could see the danger standing in front of him? I shook my head and closed my trunk as I watched him preparing to cross the street.

As much as I wanted to categorize him as just another typical guy, I couldn't. I had to accept that there was something different about him, but what that difference was I couldn't put into words. I quietly took in my defeat, jumped in my car and started pulling out of the parking spot.

To my surprise, he and his friend were still waiting to cross the street as I pulled around. He turned toward my car and this time I made sure that I caught his eyes with mine. I gave him my "It was VERY nice to meet you" squinting-smile and that pulled him right in. He took a couple of steps to my car and I happily dropped the window.

"Hey, what's your name?" He asked.

"Taylor," I responded.

Suddenly, I noticed my previous prey, the chocolate champion, step out of the store. I laughed on the inside at the ironic situation, but this type of attention comes with the Taylor Delmor package. I refocused back on the handsome stallion dying to ask me another question.

"Taylor, would you like to go grab some dinner with me tomorrow evening?"

He had already used the p-word on me once, so I had to accept. I exchanged my number for a second time that day to a new prospect and learned his name, Jacob.

Jacob seemed promising, in that he initially had been able to disregard my magnetic toxin, so maybe he was truly different. Maybe he was a lot stronger than the others.

We ended our conversation and I turned up my radio, waved and pulled off. The champion versus the stallion — what a challenge.

The second thing on my housewarming list was to do some interior décor online shopping. I decided to do that the next day. I awoke still ecstatic to be in my own place. No roommate banging pans in the kitchen in the wee morning hours. No unknown new voices, reminding me to think about what kind of clothes I needed to have on to come out of my bedroom.

Nothing.

Just the calmness of my new place. I spent the previous night entertaining my home girls and getting lost in a couple bottles of Moscato.

With a little hangover, I grabbed my phone to start my mini-shopping spree but then I noticed my phone was flashing green with several missed texts, all from unknown numbers.

> *11:25am: Area code 220: You've been on my mind since we met yesterday. I think I even dreamt about you. Are you still up for today? - Jacob*

Maybe he didn't have control like I thought…

~ 21 ~

11:32am: Area code 404: Good morning Miss Taylor. How are you doing?

11:33am: Area code 404: And just in case you forget who I am from all the attention you got yesterday this is Mason.

I was so glad Mason put his name in that last text. There were so many numbers without names in my phone already. I clicked out of my messages and focused back on my online shopping. These men in my web can wait because they have no other choice. It wasn't until 4:30pm that I remembered that I hadn't texted Jacob back.

4:32pm: It sounds like you slept well last night. :) LOL Yes I am still available for dinner tonight. Let's do 8:00 PM at the restaurant of your choice.

My phone buzzed a minute later:

4:33pm: Jacob: I'll pick you up at 7:50 PM and we can go to Remington's.

Uh no…I don't allow men to pick me up from my house on the first date. Since I knew the addiction to my presence was infectious, I wouldn't dare allow for any localized stalking.

4:34pm: I'll meet you at Remington's at 8:00 PM.

4:35pm: Jacob: Paranoid are we?

Duh…

4:36pm: Jacob: I'll see you at 8:00 PM beautiful :)

I placed my phone back on the charger and headed to my closet to pick out my "presentation" for tonight. I needed a dress that said I was sexy, but in a natural, unintentional way. I pulled out my black bow-front, low-back dress. It was a great look to accentuate the soft purple rose on my back that I usually intentionally hid from my prey. I knew the beautiful artwork that lay on my left shoulder blade would make the most faithful priest question his vow of celibacy.

Now, shoes…Christian Louboutin, Giuseppe Zanotti, or maybe a little more low-key like the Steve Maddens? I choose my strappy Jimmy Choos that a former male friend bought for me. He had great taste, but my taste for him wasn't as good.

7:45pm rolled around quickly and I prepared to walk out the door. I passed in front of my door mirror and couldn't help but rave at the finished product. I looked just right for a pleasurable night.

I pulled up in front of Remington's at 7:55pm. Remington's was an expensive, upscale restaurant. Jacob must have been into something big to get reservations here. The Valet walked up to my red mustang, took my keys and escorted me through the doors.

To my surprise, the restaurant was empty. Are they closed? Am I at the wrong location?

"Miss Taylor" the hostess introduced herself, "my name is Tami and your guest is waiting on you."

And then, it dawned on me. This man actually shut down one of the busiest and most exclusive restaurants in the city, probably on their busiest night, just for me.

Really?!
I couldn't help but question what his day job was – C-level executive, music mogul, or maybe even a benched athlete. Or, maybe it wasn't a day job I should be worried about; maybe he was a big runner in the business of "street pharmaceuticals". My mind was wandering, but I had to bring it back to the moment. The whole elaborate situation was suspicious, but I couldn't help smiling at all his effort.

I was in awe of his presentation and now dying to know what else he had up his sleeve. The pleasure principle was now in his court and I was looking forward to seeing what he would do with it.

Jacob was seated at a table by the window in a crisp navy suit jacket and a complementary button-down shirt. His jeans were pressed and his hair cut fresh.

Maybe I missed that yesterday, but I'll take it as a compliment that he took the time to get it done just for me tonight.

He greeted me with a raspy, "Good evening" as I approached the table. I don't know if it was the vibe of the evening or what, but I immediately started to feel comfortable with him; almost like I'd known him for years. This was new and scary. My excitement was building and I needed something to bring myself back down to Earth. This was just another man...or so I thought.

CLEVER

Sneaky you,

Catching my eye.

Knowing that I'm looking,

But never turning to seize your prize.

Sneaky you,

Playing the innocent role,

Knowing damn well that these thighs,

Are where you wish you could go.

Who do you think you are?

Acting like you don't see me,

Playing like this waist and this ass,

Aren't what you wished were on your T.V.

Come on kid,

It's not too much of a sin.

Let's be real!

This is the shit you wished you could live in.

Sure you may not love me now,

But just give me two rounds,

And I'll show you that this temple,

Is more than just your physical playground.

UNKNOWN VISITOR

HE STAYED TWO DOORS DOWN from me. I saw him as I walked upstairs after a long day at work; 6'2", mocha-skinned and shining from the sweat of just playing two hours of basketball at the YMCA. He carried his basketball in the crease of his muscular forearm as chiseled as the rest of his body. His cut-off Jordan shirt and shorts showed that he worked out daily, focusing on his calves, thighs and biceps.

I rushed to unlock my door so that he didn't see me dazzled by his stature. My key kept slipping past the lock as I looked up to see him walking my way. Finally able to stick my key in the lock, I looked up again and caught eyes with the gorgeous man.

His eyes searched my body, from the hair on my head to the warmth between my legs. I broke eye contact as I fell into my foyer. I regained my composure and quickly turned to watch him walk downstairs. As soon as he reached the bottom step, he looked up, as if he knew that I would be looking and boy, was he right about that!

That night as I took a shower, visions of his physique popped in and out of my mind. As the water rolled over my body, I imagined my hands were his and ran them over all the places where I wanted him. Just daydreaming of his touch caused me to come, wanting to do nothing more but to have him deep inside me.

I stepped out of the shower and heard footsteps coming up the stairs. I raced to my door to look out of the peep hole in hopes of getting another glimpse of him, but it was just those obese, loud-talking women who lived across the hall from me. *You are so dumb*, I told myself. I couldn't believe how much of an internal uproar I was making about that man. And I didn't even know his name.

As I leaned against the door, there was a sudden knock. I looked at the clock and noticed it was 10:00pm. Who was at my door at this time of night? Forgetting that I was still in my towel, I opened the door.

It was him. He paused for a minute to take notice of me standing there in front of him completely naked, besides a towel. He struggled to find his voice.

"Hey, I hate to bother you so late but, I locked myself out my apartment. Can I use your phone?"

"Sure," I replied and suddenly realized I was only wearing a towel.

"Excuse me, I don't normally answer the door like this...I mean I didn't do it because it was you...never mind just come in."

I cut my talk short, since I was putting my foot in my own mouth anyway, and gestured him through the door.

I ran to the back room and popped on a Kobe sweatshirt and some cheerleading shorts. I was rushing, so I didn't have time to put on underwear. I grabbed my cell phone and went back in the living room where he was.

"Here you go," I said, handing the cell phone out to him.

He took the phone out of my hand, lightly caressing my finger. The touch of his skin made my own skin warm up. To avoid an awkward situation, I went into the kitchen and started taking the dishes out of the dishwasher. I could hear bits and pieces of his conversation, but not anything clear. I turned to see if he was finished with my phone, when I caught him staring at me.

He quickly turned and went back to the conversation. I looked down and noticed that my shorts had risen up, showing just the lower crease of my bottom. I pulled the side down and continued to take out the dishes. I snickered to myself, surprised that he would let me catch him in the act of getting a free peek, but somehow I liked it.

What the hell? I whispered to myself. I picked up a plate and bent down completely into the dishwasher to act as if there was a dish stuck in the back. I could feel the breeze gliding through my shorts. At that moment, I knew both butt cheeks were showing, giving him more to peek at. I could feel his heated stare, as the phone conversation came to a halt.

I made sure to pause long enough for him not to memorize the details of my cove, but just enough to keep pictures popping up in his mind about how nicely shaped my ass was. I placed a glass on the shelf and glared out of my peripheral.

He quickly turned back toward the T.V. and continued his conversation, apologizing to the other person on the phone about the miscommunication and asking them to repeat what they had said. I smirked, reminding myself that I still had it. About ten more minutes passed and I was sitting in my chair when he finished his phone conversation.

"Thank you. My cousin is going to come by with the spare key. He lives right down the street from here." He told me.

I was a little saddened to know that he was leaving, but satisfied that he was able to get back into his apartment, even though he was more than welcome to stay here with me in my bed for however long he wanted. I escorted him to my door, opening it slowly for him. He walked up close to me, face to face.

It was as if he wanted to kiss me and knew I wanted him to, but he only replied, "Thank you again and I'll see you around." I couldn't believe it. My body wanted him so bad, but there was no way that he wanted the same thing, or so I thought.

A couple of days passed and I did not see the stranger. I stayed attentive to who was walking past my door, but he was never there when I looked out my peep hole. My mind and body were disappointed. I plotted out in my mind that the next time that I saw him, I would be bold and ask him out. He had to have felt the vibe that was circling us.

I got myself ready for bed, and plopped down to watch a midnight episode of House. Before the second commercial break, I was asleep. I was dreaming about a paradise rendezvous with my mystery man when I heard arguing outside my apartment. I got up, slid on my comfy house shoes and slowly walked over to the door to be nosey. I looked through my peep hole to see my mystery man and a woman in a yelling match. I couldn't really make out what they were saying outside of the "shits," "damns" and "fuck-yous."

She was crying and he was gritting his teeth. It was weird, because his gritting turned me on. She ran up to him and tried to give him a hug, but he pushed her off and told her to leave. My mind was racing, trying to figure out what could have caused such a horrible argument? Did she say the wrong thing?

Did she get caught in the wrong? Maybe, she had been caught cheating.

What a dummy, I whispered to myself. *How could any woman want to do a man like that wrong? What was her problem? Maybe she was blind, or just plain dumb.* The woman yelled one more "Fuck you" and stomped down the stairs. I could hear her opening and slamming her car door furiously. I put my attention back on him and watched as his face turned from total anger, to being distraught, almost as if the air had been taken from his lungs. I opened the door slowly and looked to the right and then to the left at him.

"Is everything ok?"

"Yeah", he looked up at me, "Everything is better now. I had to clean house and get my shit right. Sorry about all that commotion."

"It's cool. I was just worried that someone was caught breaking into an apartment or something."

He laughed a little and the tension in the air lightened up just a tad.

"Well I just wanted to check on everything. I was worried about you...I mean...I was worried about what was going on out here. Let me know if you need anything, ok?"

I was hoping that he missed my stumble in words.

"Thank you," he said with a quick grin, "I appreciate that. Really I do, but I'm going to head back inside. Not feeling the greatest right now."

He started to walk back to his apartment when I blurted out, "Please let me know if you need anything, even if it is just a shoulder to lean on."

He nodded and proceeded to walk through his door.

I questioned myself, wondering if I shouldn't have laid the sympathy on so thick, but I didn't regret it. He looked like he needed a friend, at least for that moment. I closed the door and headed back to my bedroom to finish my slumber. I couldn't have been more than five minutes into my sleep when I heard a hard bang on my door.

I quickly got up and grabbed the bat that sat right next to my bed. As I slowly walked to my door, I mapped out a quick escape plan in case it was a late night attacker. The plan included jumping off my living room balcony, which I knew wouldn't hurt too much since I was just on the second floor. *Yeah that would work.*

I peeked out the peephole expecting to see some scary, and possibly masked, stranger but it was just my sexy, intriguing stranger/neighbor from downstairs in a wife-beater that exposed the beautiful artistry on his shoulders, arms and chest. He was such a masterpiece.

"Hey," I said as I opened the door.

"Hey, I know it's late," he apologized.

I turned to the clock to see that it was 3:55am.

"But I know that you said I could come by if I just needed a shoulder."

I shook my head, agreeing to what I'd said.

"But I need a little more than just a shoulder," he added. At the end of that statement, he looked right into my eyes.

My heart began to beat faster, wondering if he was going to say what my thighs had been yearning for him to say every time I saw him. He took a couple steps toward me, standing close enough for me to smell the remnants of a mint.

"I need...I mean, I want...some of you."

My eyes widened as I stood without breathing. He moved in to kiss my lips and I don't know what came over me, but I took a step back from him. His movement forward ceased, as if he had just reached the edge of a cliff and was about to jump off with his next step.

"I'm sorry. I can't." My mouth spoke, as my body shivered from the idea of his with mine. "I'm not sure what to make of this. I mean, I don't even know your name."

"You're right...I'm...I'm so sorry. I'm just going to go home."

Before I could catch the words that had just come out my mouth, he was away from my door and back into his apartment.

I couldn't believe myself. All this time I've been fantasizing about this man and the one time I could have had just a small piece of him, I threw it away. And for what? Pride...ego...sheer stupidity?

What are you doing? I whispered to myself.

I was trying to be good and do the right thing, at least in society's eyes. I didn't want to take advantage of him in his weakened state, but maybe that's just what he needed. Maybe society was wrong on this one.

And then I made my final decision. I left my head back in my apartment as my body and heart went to his door and started knocking. He opened it slowly.

"I'm sorry...I'm not sure what just happened but...I'm here if you need or just want me...but don't get it twisted...I mean..." my words came out in a blur.

By this time, I was surely feeling like I had left both my brain and head back in my apartment. I continued to fumble through my words as he walked into me, shutting me up with the warmth of his lips around mine. Every word I was thinking disappeared as I closed my eyes to enjoy the moment.

His lips were just right, large enough to control our movements and gentle enough for me to yearn for more. He grabbed my waist and pulled me closer, inserting his tongue in my mouth and massaging mine with his. I let out a small moan.

I couldn't wait any longer. I pushed him back with my hands. He took a step back and dropped his head, confused about what I was doing to him. If only he knew!

Hell, I was just getting started. . .

I grabbed his hand and led him up the stairs, and to my door. We walked in and as I closed the door, he grabbed me from behind and began to kiss on my neck. I slowly closed and locked the door. The blood flowing in my veins rushed to my thighs. His kiss was wet but soothing. As he circled around the left side of my neck, he went to pull my shirt over my head. I assisted him, yanking my shirt off to show my two butterfly tattoos on my naked back.

He proceeded to move my hair over my shoulder and kissed me from the top of my neck, down my spine, to the top of my ass. I used my hands to keep myself balanced on the door.

Each kiss he gave me made me reach higher on the door, stretching my back out so he could taste every bit of my longing skin. He removed my shorts slowly and carefully, ensuring that he saw every ounce of my apple. His hands firmly massaged my ankles, my calves and caressed the seam of my ass. He kissed and rubbed each cheek as if he were formally introducing himself to them. I dropped my head down to let out more moans. His kisses and touch warmed my sweet center at an accelerated rate.

As I dropped my head in front of me, I opened my eyes to see his hand rubbing my inner thigh and then caressing the juicy spot between my legs. My legs unlocked for a second as my muscles relaxed. He flicked my clit with his thumb as he dipped his fingers in and out of me.

Never had I felt this type of pleasure before and I prayed that it would never stop. He only entered me several times with his fingers before he moved directly under me, preparing to feast on his early morning snack. I opened my eyes to make sure I was feeling the same tongue that enthroned my mouth, as we met eye-to-eye. I watched him close his eyes, as if he were memorizing the inside of me with his tongue. His hands held me up as my legs were completely gone from the overflow of arousal. He used me as if I was his gorge; savoring every ounce he could of me. I moaned louder and louder.

"It feels so good." I told him.

"Uh huh," was all he could say, as he had me to keep his mouth full.

The vibration from his words shocked my core. I wanted to find a way to grip the wall to brace for the incoming release, but I couldn't. My body tensed up, making me let out a long and strong moan of "yes". I came hard. His tongue and those words were all I needed. My knees buckled, seeking some sort of strength. I needed more.

I took a few more rejuvenating breaths and regained feeling and strength back into my legs just in time for him to guide me from the door to the couch, bending me forward.

He slowly reached in his pants and pulled out his staff, gently rubbing my behind with it – rekindling my inferno for another round. I reached as far as I could over the couch and straddled myself, showing him that I was ready to take it all and he immediately understood. The pressure of his mass inside of me caused me to yelp and whine, but I made sure not to tense up too much. With each stroke he stretched my cove, hitting my g-spot. I didn't know that mine existed until that moment. He was breathing new life into my senses. I grabbed the couch cushions and buried my head to keep the moans from getting louder.

"Please, don't hide them from me. I want to hear you scream." His voice was soothing and erotic all at the same time.

I granted him his wish and began to free up my moans. Each moan caused him to drive deeper. I lifted my right leg, so he could angle himself just right inside of me. Together we moaned and thrust against each other.

"Don't stop, please don't." I begged.

I knew I was within seconds from reaching my peak. His thrusts were rapid and steady. I grabbed for some air and let out the sweetest moan that made him lose control. He pulled out still dripping with our juices and proceeded to come on my back.

I opened my eyes to feel him rubbing his shaft up and down between my legs. I collapsed over the back of the couch until he whispered in my ear, "Let's go to bed."

He picked my exhausted body up and carried me into my bedroom. We got into bed and he must have recouped on the way back to my bedroom, because we went at it again.

After two more times, we laid naked and exhausted in my now sheet-less bed. He held me in his arms and kissed my forehead softly. We began to drift off to sleep when I remembered there was something I needed to ask him.

"Hey, hon," I whispered to him.

"Yeah?"

"What's your name?"

THE PLEASURE PRINCIPLE:

Part II

REMINGTON'S WAS A ROMANTIC restaurant with low lighting and an intimate ambiance. Add that to Jacob's flawless first-date presentation and I was definitely in unexpected shock and awe. After about ten minutes, I was able to calm myself and settle into the dinner. Jacob and I talked about everything; from our hometowns just a couple of hours away from each other in Florida, to our career aspirations.

He was a successful entrepreneur who owned several small businesses and franchised several 24-hour Gyms throughout the city. We even debated a little bit about where we wanted to see our lives go; world traveling, marriage, kids, the whole shebang.

Before dessert arrived, I decided to take a quick break to the restroom. With purse in hand, I strolled to the back, searching for the powder room. As I peeked around the corner, I realized that there was music playing overhead throughout the restaurant.

Maxwell's "Sumthing, Sumthing" was humming through the speakers and I couldn't help but wonder if he also planned that out. A subtle message, but I could hear it. Then I felt my phone vibrate in my purse. I took it out to see two missed text messages and one voicemail.

Missed call: Mason

Missed messages:

8:35pm: Mason: Miss Taylor, I don't mean to bother you but can I take you out tonight?

8:45pm: Mason: I hope it's not too late. But if it is can I see you tomorrow?

Mason seemed very determined to get my attention and for some odd reason it jump started my curiosity. Do I dare? The audacity of me! But what the hell, right?

10:12pm: I'm just seeing your message but I could do something tonight. Since it's so late, what about a hookah bar or lounge?

10:15pm: Mason: We can do a hookah bar. I know a great one downtown, Mila's.

I was very familiar with Mila's. I had a standing monthly date with my girls there.

10:16pm: Sounds great. I can meet you at 11:30 pm.

~ 43 ~

I made sure to push the time back as far as possible to ensure that I could change from my sexy formal first date dress to a flirty but relaxed jumpsuit.

I stopped for a moment, realizing that I was planning to end this great date with this wonderful man with absolutely no plans of passing on pleasure. Maybe he wasn't as appealing as I thought he was. Maybe the lust was there, but my mind wasn't. Maybe he was too much of a gentleman. Confused at my inability to curve my appetite for one man, I quickly used the bathroom, mentally rehearsing my getaway excuse.

I walked back out, noticing that our table was gone and he was now standing in the middle of a vacant floor, waiting for me.

"So…" he paused, "can I have this dance?" I thought it was very cliché, taken straight from some romance movie, but it was still sweet. I politely smiled and met him with open arms. He pulled me in close, tightly wrapping his arms around my waist.

"Thank you again."

"For what, this time?" I asked.

"For making this the best night I've had in a really long time. You're such a pleasure to be around and..." He paused for a second "You're absolutely perfect."

His words made me rethink my second date. But then my paranoia came back. I thought about how many women he had probably done this for. Was that "game" he'd just thrown at me? Was I just another mark to add to his bed post? Hell, this is Atlanta. The men-to-woman ratio alone was like one straight man to twenty straight women.

I suddenly used his kind words against him and proceeded with my excuse.

"You know what, Jacob?" I stopped our dance in mid-step. "This is going too fast for me. I mean you pull out this hat trick on me by closing down a restaurant and then tell me everything I've ever wanted to hear just after meeting me a day ago. I mean, come on…"

He took a step back from me with a confused and semi-pissed face.

"Come on what? I wanted to impress you…is that a bad thing? I mean, you didn't seem like just another woman, so I show you that you're not and you get upset by it?"

I tried my best not to give in and apologize. The pleasure of the moment was drifting and I didn't want to hurt his feelings. I just wanted to get away. But it did make me wonder why I couldn't stick with this good guy.

I began to change my tactics.

"Ok. I'll be honest. I think this was an absolutely perfect night; almost too perfect and that scares me. I'm not the type of girl who men normally wine and dine because I don't allow them to. But, somehow you snuck it up on me. I don't want this to end badly, but this is a lot for me to take in. Can we end this night with a kiss and some time for me to digest it all? You're amazing and it has also been my pleasure to spend this time with you but I need time. This is so new to me."

His frustrated demeanor changed back into the calm, smiling man that I had just had dinner with, again showing me his beautiful smile and making me take unconscious steps toward him. Before I knew it, we were in a deep and long kiss. Our lips fell perfectly onto one another. His hands drew my body in closer to him, lightly grazing the top of my bottom, but not racing to cup the full thing. He was such a gentleman.

I ended the kiss abruptly, noticing that my desire to give pleasure was growing and I had to stop the feeling.

I made sure we locked eyes and then whispered "Thank you" to him before I grabbed my purse and headed to the door.

Before exiting, I turned around to see that he was shooting down his full drink. I expected him to be a little rattled by my swift departure, but he wasn't.

He just tipped his head to me with that gorgeous smile, as if to say, "I understand" and then he turned to head to the back.

Now, I was the confused one. He just took it so calmly and I couldn't figure out why. Was he just that nice of a guy? Or, was this all part of some master plan? It was evident that my poison was working, but his was, too.

I rushed home so I could hurry and get dressed to meet Mason. The bar/club I was meeting him at was very low- key. Men wore jeans and graphic tees and women did the "casual cute" look, pairing jeans with raunchy tops or vice versa. So, I decided to trade in the short dress for some short black shorts – cut short enough for some lucky guy to take a peek at my cheeks if I dropped something. And, I matched it with a plaid red and black button down shirt. I pulled my hair up in a bun and grabbed some Jordan's from my closet. It was the opposite feel from what I just had on, but the sexy factor still remained evident. I grabbed my keys and ran to my car.

The place was only five minutes away, so even though I was late, it was only by ten minutes. I looked to see if he was there and didn't see him. I walked over to the bar and grabbed a seat. I took out my phone to text him.

11:42pm: I'm here. Where are you?

As I waited for him to text back the bartender asked me what I wanted and I ordered a Vodka and cranberry. Then I felt my phone buzz.

11:44pm: Mason: I'm running late but I'll be there in like five minutes.

My attitude sharply changed. Strike one. As I sat there impatiently waiting, I took a moment to people-watch. The club was made up of a diverse group – singles and couples, black, white, Asian and others. The deep pockets had their own section with people filled to the max – women sitting and men standing. The other men were positioned strategically around the bar and the dance floor, scouting out potential conquests.

I was turning back to the bar when I caught the eye of a very sexy, smooth-skinned man. His facial hair was giving me Brad Pitt, but his smile was definitely more David Beckham. He nodded at me and I nodded back, provoking him to come to me.

Let the poisoning begin.

Right as I was prepping myself for his intro, I heard over the speakers: "Look who just walked in. My man Mason Deeds! Whattup boi!"

I turned quickly to the door to see that the Mason that I was waiting on was the same being announced.

He saluted the deejay and started searching the crowd. I noticed he had a few people with him, including a female.

Really? I thought to myself.

He finally looked over to the bar and saw me. He immediately smiled and began pushing through the crowd. His announcement made me wonder whether he had deep pockets, or did he just club too much. I totally forgot about my Pitt-Beckham guy until he tapped my shoulder.

"Hi," Pitt-Beckham said with his beautiful smile.

"Hey man. What's going on?" Mason responded, quickly grabbing his hand before I could even reach out.

I couldn't do anything but laugh on the inside and observe how he would handle this situation. Where was a bag of popcorn when you needed it?

"I really wish we could stay, Man, but we…" Mason grabbed my hand, ushering me from the chair "…have to go."

Pitt-Beckham just nodded and gave a smirk before diving back into his cup.

I gave a friendly wave good-bye and followed Mason into the crowd. He guided me to a small section, tucked toward the back of the club, but still close to the dance floor. Once we sat down, I waited to see if the others that had come in with him would join us, but they didn't.

"Where's your entourage?" I asked.

"Who?"

"The group of people you came in with."

"Oh no," He answered, "those are just some friends of mine that met me here to get in. I got this section for us."

"Really…why?"

I thought it was weird to have to have bottles and all that space just for two people.

"Well, it's the only space in the spot that I can have you to my own," he paused. "And get you drunk."

We both laughed.

"I'm only joking," he stated, but I know he probably wasn't.

"So who are you? I mean do you always get announced when stepping in here?" I asked.

"Well. . ." He poured himself a drink and took a sip before answering. "This is my spot. I own it. Well, me and my brother own it. And, as much as I tell them don't shout me out, they still do it to embarrass me."

I was a little shocked. Did I really just meet two men who were doing great things for themselves? I nodded to him and took a sip from the wine glass the waitress poured for me.

"So, what have you been up to today?" He asked.

I smiled and took another sip. I have a motto: lying is for the lazy and truthfulness is for the powerful. So, I told him the truth.

"Well...I cleaned up my house, washed my car, went on a date, got dressed to come here..."

"Wait." He stopped me. "You went on a date tonight?"

I took another sip, hoping that the liquor would take control quicker, but it didn't.

"Yep and it was a good guy too."

"Let me guess – the guy from the grocery store?"

"How did you know?"

"Oh. It was just a good guess. But go on. 'He was a good guy' and what else?"

I wasn't expecting him to want to continue the conversation but I went on.

"It was nice...very nice. But I was also wondering about you. So, that's when I answered your text."

He fell silent for several moments, making for a tense and awkward mood shift. *Here we go*, I thought to myself. At least I was being honest.

"So, did I win?" He finally asked.

"Did you win what, exactly?"

"You."

He turned to look at me, making sure to keep constant eye contact as I searched for the words to answer.

I shyly looked away and answered, "It's not a contest. I just decided to see what else was out there. But who knows…maybe he will win in the end."

I couldn't believe that I just threw a jab after an upper cut. I guess I was just curious about how far I could push him before he was like, "nice knowing you", but it didn't seem like it was going to work.

"Well I'll make sure that I'm the last one standing in the end. No worries."

His comment was egotistical and so sexy. I began wondering if he was under my spell, or if it was it me now who was falling in a trance.

Suddenly, a waitress appeared from the back and whispered into his ear. She seemed a little frantic, but of course his calm, mellow self just quietly spoke back to her and then turned to me.

"My apologies, but I have to go handle something real quick. Will you stay and wait on me? Maybe even finish this bottle."

I poured myself a glass and gestured to him to go ahead. He smoothly grabbed my hand and placed a warm kiss on the top. And as he got up, he moved in to give me an even warmer kiss on my neck.

I felt a chill go down my body. He was now in control and I was anticipating the pleasure that could follow. As I sat and waited for him to come back I felt my phone buzz.

12:30am: Jacob: I know it's late but I just wanted to check and make sure you made it home safely.

I had completely forgotten to text him and there was no way I was lying to him now, so I voted against communicating back. No harm, no foul; right?

Thirty minutes passed, the bottle was empty and I was down to my last glass. As if on cue, Mason came back and sat next to me.

"I'm glad to see that no one stole you from me this time."

"No one stole me from you the first time. I just needed to know if you were interested."

"Oh I am *very* interested." He turned to me and bit his lip.

I could feel my leg start shaking, almost like it was revving my body up for something.

"It's time to slow it down one time" the deejay yelled from his perch. Then R. Kelly's *Bump-n-Grind* blew through the speakers.

It was as if R's voice had put a spell on body. I stood up and starting rocking to the beat; snapping and singing, 'I don't see nothing wrooonggg' as the whole mood of the lounge slowed down.

Soon Mason got up behind me, swaying to the lyrics and whispering in my ear, ". . .with a little bump and grind."

Maybe it was the wine, or maybe my body was just ready to give in to some pleasure, but I took my time rocking my hips into him and pulling his arms around my waist.

He pulled me closer to him with each sway, so it was almost like no one was in the room.

We slowed our rocking further, literally warming up each other's body through our clothes.

Right as the song was going off, Mason sweetly whispered in my ear, "Are you ready to go?"

Was I?

I guessed so, seeing that the song was over, but the mood was still right. I did question myself for a moment, wondering if I was truly intrigued by him, or still desiring Jacob. I wasn't sure, but he was there and I was interested…so why not? The selfish part of me wanted to have them both, but since I couldn't, at least one would be pleasurable.

"Sure." I confidently replied back and before I could even grab my purse he was calling the car around at the front door.

He assured me that the parking lot had 24-hour surveillance, so my car would be safe for the night. We hopped in his car and sped off to his condo, which was right down the block. Even on the short ride, I couldn't help but think again about the kind and understanding man that I met with earlier that day.

He was totally opposite from Mason. Mason was over-confident and even came on strong at times. Jacob seemed more reserved, but such a gentleman. I was second-guessing my choice. I pulled out my phone quickly.

> *1:32am: I'm so sorry I missed your message but I'm good and I hope to see you again soon.*

My thoughts started to race, wondering why I was allowing the bad boy to take precedence over the good guy.

We pulled up to the 5th Hotel and he ushered me upstairs. As he stood next to me in the elevator, I could feel the mood shift again. The body that was once excited was now confused and a little off-track. The elevator door opened and we walked into this amazing high-rise condo decked out in black and stainless-steel furniture. The paintings on the wall came from the Harlem Renaissance painter Aaron Douglas.

As I walked further into the main room, I saw old pictures of what I assumed to be family hanging on the wall. They were beautiful and well-kept. It made me wonder how old they were. As I awed over their flawless grade, I noticed that the photos showed an array of complexions from dark-rich to creamy-white tones.

"Those are my great-great-grandparents and my cousins." he blurted out.

"Forgive me if this comes off weird," I started in, "but are you mixed?" My curiosity got the best of me and I needed more details behind the images I was admiring.

"No. But my brothers are. I have two and we all have the same mother with different dads. My mother is mixed – Irish, black and Jamaican. She married my dad, who is black. Her skin is very fair, nearly white. I got my dad's complexion. One of my brother's father is mixed, black and white, so his skin is much lighter than mine and my older brother's dad is Italian, so he really looks like a white guy."

"Wow. You have a rainbow family." I smiled at him, but then realized that my comment probably came off very cheesy and even kid-ish.

"Yeah, we are a rainbow. Can I grab you a drink?"

"I'll take some water, please. But can I use your restroom first."

"Sure. Let me walk you to it."

The hall leading the bathroom was full of more photos — family photos I assumed. And then there it was. Just a couple steps from the bathroom door, I saw Mason in a photo…next to Jacob!

I stopped to fully examine the picture and make sure my eyes weren't playing tricks on me.

"Is something wrong?" he asked.

Then I realized that shit just got real. I snapped back toward him doing my best to not look as agitated as I felt.

"No, no. I'm good. No really, I'm good."

"Ok" he answered but I could tell he knew something was up.

"I was just admiring your family and then my head started pounding." I threw my hand on my forehead hoping I gave a convincing act.

"Oh. Do you need something like Tylenol or...?"

I cut him off. "No, no. Hopefully it will pass. Thanks for showing me to the bathroom. I'll be right out."

I walked past him quickly. Right before I closed the door I mentally took a jump.

"Hey!" I yelled at him.

"Yeah, what's up?"

"Who's that guy in the photo with you?"

"Which one? This one?" He pointed to the targeted photo.

"Yeah."

"That's my brother Jacob."

I smiled and closed the door.

What...the...shit? I told myself in the mirror. Out of all the men in city, I had decided to date brothers in the same damn night. And not only that, I liked them both. I dropped my head and whispered to myself again, *What...the...shit? Pull it together. You got this. YOU...GOT...THIS.*

I shook the fear and confusion right out of me. Who was I kidding? I'm mother-fucking Taylor Eliza Delmor. I'm in control: I hold the key. I AM the pleasure principle. My self-pep talk got me hyped and I used the bathroom and walked back out feeling totally in control and focused on ending my night how I planned.

"Thought you'd got lost," he joked.

I gave him that "whatever" grin and met him at the kitchen bar where my glass was waiting.

"So..." I started, prepped to show myself how much control I had. "Where's your room?"

He smiled and took a sip. Without any words he grabbed my hand and walked me to the opposite side of the room. Then we heard the door unlock and open.

In walked Jacob. REALLY!? Shocked just didn't describe his look.

"Hey Man, what's up?" Mason walked over to Jacob and gripped him up.

Jacob never took his eyes off me. The confidence that I had just pumped myself up with diminished. I was left feeling disgusted at myself and confused on how to get myself out of the room. How does this look to him? I mean, I just found out that they were brothers.

Jacob finally took his eyes off me as Mason started to introduce me. "Hey, this is Taylor. Taylor this is my brother – the one I just told you about."

I felt a little better when he said, "I just told you about" out loud. Maybe Jacob would have mercy on me; I didn't know. But I just knew it didn't matter — he probably didn't believe it and I couldn't blame him.

"Nice to see you again," Jacob responded.

"Again, huh?" Now Mason was staring at me, but not with a shocked face, more of a smirk.

And before I could even say anything, Jacob chimed in. "I'm going to head off to bed. Y'all have a good night."

And he was gone. As awkward as the situation had started, it quickly ended. The emotions I felt were mixed. I was disappointed that I was in this position, but inquisitive on how this would end with both of them. Yes, my selfish self still hoped for some time with Jacob, even if it was just to apologize and walk away. I couldn't let us end like this: he was too good of a guy.

Mason turned around and continued to pull me to his room but the mood had definitely shifted. I sat on his bed and threw my head to hands.

"So. . ." he started, "you've met Jacob before?"

I shook my head yes, totally embarrassed by the truth.

"And let me guess, that's who you went on a date with before you came and saw me?"

Here we go, I thought to myself, quietly planning my getaway, eyeing how far my purse was from the door.

"This is too funny! Now it all makes sense." He was actually laughing. Not mad, but laughing at the situation. "He came in here tonight saying that he met the perfect woman, but when I drilled him about seeing her again, he said he didn't know. Said she seemed to be looking for something else."

But, that was the farthest from the truth: I wasn't looking for something else. I just wanted to keep my options open just like a man would do. I do like Jacob; I just like Mason, too.

"So now what?" Mason sat down on the bed next to me. He didn't seem bothered, but was more attentive to how I was. Hell, he probably thought he'd won, so let's continue.

"You know what, I think this is too much. I didn't know y'all were related and as much as it looks like I'm trying to get over on you two, I'm not. You're both good guys and honestly, if I could have you both I would but…" I pushed away from him and grabbed my purse. "…I'm just going to leave."

"What if you can?"

"What if I can, what?" I replied, with purse now in hand.

"What if you could have us both…at least sexually for one night?"

I was totally confused by this point. "So, you're saying you want to run a train on me with your brother?"

"No. I'm saying I want to give you what you want. And I'm sure he wouldn't mind sharing you for one night."

I turned and faced him. "Are you shitting me?" My response came out crazy but I felt it was perfect for that crazy-ass situation.

"I'll be right back. Please don't go yet." He left the room.

I was trying to digest what was going on, but my mind was just all over the place. Jacob had said I was "the perfect woman". Why is this all so funny to Mason? Why would Mason ever agree to something like this? Was I getting set up by a pair of brothers, waiting to get me into a compromising position and then trashing me?

~ 61 ~

Or, was this really about to happen? Was I going to get what I wanted after all – both of them?

I turned and walked toward his window. The skyline of the city was bright. Through the darkness, lights glimmered from nearby businesses, streets and towers. There was so much life still going in the city at this late hour; so much opportunity still left in the night. So, was I going to miss this one?

I heard the door open, but I couldn't move. I had no idea what to expect so I decided to freeze up.

"It would be my pleasure," Jacob's voice resounded as he got closer.

Then, I felt a hand — his, I assumed, on my waist and then the warmth of his breath on my neck. My anticipation immediately started rising.

"For one night, I'll share you," he whispered to me.

My heart was beating through my chest and reverberating throughout my body. Then I felt a hand touch my hand.

It was Mason again, pulling me back to the bed. Jacob's hand intertwined with the other, following us to bed.

I had so many questions. I was still so confused, but my body took over my mind's concerns. Another twinge of fear stepped in the back of my mind, as I still wondered if this was a set-up.

Mason sat me on the bed with Jacob's assistance in leaning me back.

"Are you ready?" Mason asked.

I had no answer.

Jacob placed his lips on mine and I closed my eyes. I could feel my shorts being unfastened and slowly pulled over my thighs.

"I didn't know..." I started to tell my side of the story to Jacob, but he was no longer interested.

"It doesn't matter. I have you now." Jacob's kisses moved around my neck and then down my chest.

Mason was starting from the opposite direction, kissing my toes, then my calves up to the inner thighs. My blood was like fire coursing through my veins, heating up all my pleasurable zones. My body was ready, wetting up and gearing up for the ride of my life.

I didn't know what do with my hands. Should I pull Mason's head closer or search for Jacob's staff? So many options. And then Mason dove in deep, darting his tongue in and out of me, around me, and up and down me. I grabbed a pillow to put my face in, doing my best to quiet my moans and momentary screams.

"Excuse me. Can I have that?"

Jacob was now reaching for the pillow with his mass out and standing at attention.

It was time for the pleasure principle to take control. I sat up slightly and began to kiss it slowly and softly, knowing that each kiss was a tease to his ultimate massacre. I licked around the tip and then up and down the shaft. Then, I did my best to take it all in my mouth, but he was too large. I could hear his groans. They made me look directly up his flawless abs into his eyes, wanting him to see how much I enjoyed pleasuring him.

While still on my back, Mason brought my attention back to him. With condom perfectly attached, he thrust his mass inside me. His girth wasn't as large as Jacob's, but his length was unmatched.

Then, it became a tennis match: Jacob, who was now directly over me feeding me all of him, was competing with his brother, who was deep inside of me, stretching and hitting my g-spot. I was full and enjoying it. My moans soon grew over theirs. Every erotic point on my body was now heading to peak. I could feel myself preparing for what I hoped was the first of multiple climatic moments in this night.

They were giving more pleasure than I ever could have asked for. I didn't care about having control anymore; I only wanted more and more of them. I couldn't get enough. And then…the door flew open.

It was the Pitt-Beckham guy. We all stopped but neither exited me.

"Wow. My bad," he stated.

"You're good, big bro," Mason replied.

Big bro!?

Could this really be freaking true?

I ran into ALL three brothers tonight.

"Cool, cool, cool. Hey, can I join?" He began taking off his shirt showing off his lightly-tanned, eight pack.

Well… I thought to myself, *you can never have too much pleasure…right?*

OFFICE EXTRAVAGANZA

"I'LL LOCK THE DOOR when I leave. . .don't worry about it," I yelled to Dora, the operations manager.

"Thanks, Nat. You're the greatest," she responded.

I had decided to stay as long as it took to complete my dashboards. I walked back to my reception desk and unlocked my screen to notice that I had an IM up.

Marc: *You still here too?*

It was the new guy. He was working late on his first week — poor baby.

Natalie: *Yeah. They work me to the bone every day.*

Marc: *Man, they're tough here. How do you do it?*

Natalie: *I just do it. Like Nike.*

Marc: *LOL. Yeah I like that motto, in more than one way.*

I sat back and wondered exactly what he meant. How many ways could you just do it? Was he flirting with me?

Marc was the new IT manager brought in to help with our computer chaos. He seemed quiet, even shy at times. Most of the ladies thought he was cute; twenty-six years old, five/ten with caramel skin. He was alright. Okay, maybe a little cute. Let me stop fronting; he was *hot*. It was the first time in a while that the office had had some eye-candy, but he was definitely delicious to the eyes.

Marc: *Hello!*

Natalie: *My bad, I just got a phone call.*

I lied because I didn't want him to know that I was trying to figure out his comment.

Natalie: *What are you up to this weekend?*

Marc: *I'll probably go play some ball and then chill at home. Maybe do some cooking.*

Natalie: *Oh you cook? Go ahead! I don't know too many men that can cook.*

Marc: *Oh I cook, girl. I do it well, just like other things.*

All the innuendos were starting to add up: I was sure he was being flirtatious now. I crossed my legs and moved a little closer to my computer screen.

Marc: *What do you like to eat?*

Natalie: *I love seafood, especially crab legs.*

Marc: *I'm not really a seafood person, but I do love fish. I'll try anything twice. I have a thing about having different textures on my tongue.*

My mind shifted to wondering how much he would like the taste of me. What am I doing? Jon was at home. At this moment, cooking dinner waiting on me to join him. I refocused my mind and shifted the conversation.

Natalie: *So, are you watching the game this weekend?*

Marc: *Yeah, but I think I'm going to come in this weekend and do a little work.*

Natalie: *Yeah, I think I am too, because I need a head start on some projects for next week.*

I thought it was a little funny how we both felt the need to come in and work on the weekend.

Not too many other people in the office like that idea at all, but I usually do. I have a key and pass-code for every door in the building.

> Natalie: *I'm coming in the afternoon on Saturday. If you want to come then I can let you in.*
>
> Marc: *Sounds good. See you at 1:00 on Saturday.*

I was just getting back from a five-day vacation, so I had only been in the office three times since he started. Marc was a nice, hardworking guy. He had a genuine smile and spoke to everyone; even the "I hate my job every day" grouchy people. It was refreshing to have someone else around who seemed to be as calm as I was.

On the ride home that night, I was thinking about whether or not we had everything for dinner, when my mind slipped back to the IM conversation I'd had with Marc. I could just hear his soothing, mellow voice speak those words to me: *"I have a thing about having different textures on my tongue."*

I felt a little moisture develop between my legs. Could I be attracted to Marc? *Hell yeah, who wouldn't be?* I told myself as I pulled up to my apartment complex.

The next day, I woke a little later than intended. Jon and I stayed up all night playing Wii and watching a late-night fright-fest movie.

I got up and threw on my black workout gauchos with a bra and a zip-up hoodie. Then, I suddenly remembered that I was supposed to meet Marc at the office at 1 pm and it was 12:30pm.

"Shit!" I yelled out loud.

"What's wrong?" Jon asked

"Nothing; just running behind."

I grabbed my purse and keys, kissed Jon goodbye and raced out the door. I yelled back to him that I would see him later and hopped in my car.

There wasn't any traffic on the road, so I actually made it there at the same time Marc was pulling up. He had on a University of Michigan cut-off shirt and some gray sweat pants, sagging just a little below his waist so I could see his gray and navy boxers.

"Hey, Pretty Lady," he said, smiling at me.

"Hey, Sir," I spoke while typing in the code.

He quickly got in front of me and opened the door. I appreciated that he believed in chivalry, so I thanked him.

As I passed in front of him, we caught eyes. I looked into his eyes and saw something I hadn't noticed before. In those eyes I saw a spark, some glimpse of what he probably had already planned out in his mind; something a little lustful.

I quickly broke eye contact, realizing that it was causing me to walk slowly, like a scene straight out of a romance movie. I did my rendition of a speed-walk race over to the elevators and hit the "up" button. He followed me at his usual pace into the elevator.

I pushed the "8" button and we stood there waiting for our arrival to the requested floor. His Sean John cologne enticed all my senses at once. The intertwined heat from his body and the smell of his cologne caused the hairs on the back of my neck to stand up.

From my peripheral glance, I saw he was looking at me and for some reason, I enjoyed it.

The bell rang and the doors opened to let us out. I unlocked the office door. Like he did downstairs, he opened it, but this time slowly, to make sure that I took my time walking past him. As I started into the office, I could have sworn I felt his eyes follow my apple-shaped bottom. Was he wondering how juicy it may be? I stopped at my desk and he continued down the hall to his office. I got myself together, sat down and began to start up my CPU. About thirty minutes passed before he began to IM me.

Marc: *How's it going up there?*

Natalie: *Pretty good. Actually I'm almost done.*

Marc: *Hey, can I ask you a question?*

Natalie: Yeah what's up?

Marc: Are you attracted to me?

I read the message a total of five times trying to figure out how to answer the question. I couldn't believe he just came out like that. The nerve of that man.

Natalie: What? How are you going to ask me something like that?

Marc: I mean no offense. I'm just really attracted to you and I was wondering if you were feeling the same thing too.

The IM on my screen caught me off-guard; not because he actually sent the message, but because of my answer. I was attracted to him, but I couldn't tell him so. Jon and I had been together for close to three years, now. He was a great guy and things were looking pretty good. I even thought that this year would be the year he pops the question, so why would I mess that up?

Marc sent me another message before I could even respond.

Marc: I mean you have the prettiest smile and your skin reminds me of silk – perfectly smooth and soft. All I really want to do is just touch it once and see if it feels the same.

I took a moment to lean in closer to the screen, anticipating his next message.

Marc: I hope I'm not coming on too strong but I've been thinking about you since we first met. Your exotic grayish-green eyes and plump lips were the first things to catch my eye.

His compliments caught me off-guard and caused me to back slowly away from the screen, re-crossing my legs again and feeling the warmth and moisture begin to form at my cove.

I was shocked at his bold manner, but also very turned on. It was different from Jon's tactics — very straight forward and risky. It was interesting to see another man respond to me — even a little confusing — but my curiosity was piqued.

Natalie: Wow! I wasn't expecting that. I mean you're a handsome guy and you seem to have your head on straight. I mean you are a hard worker and all but. . .

Marc: Babe, hardworking is just a part of me. Right now the only hard work I want to do is on you, from the nips of your ears to the bottom of your feet. I want to work to satisfy you.

Wow, he is not playing, I thought. I switched my legs as the wetness was now very noticeable. I could feel my skin and my hands heating up, as if I was sitting on a beach about to jump into the ocean. But, my current ocean was in the form of Marc's mass.

> Marc: *You're so beautiful and all I can think about is what you would look like stepping out the shower and then lying on my bed. Please forgive me but I can't help myself. No disrespect to your man.*

No disrespect huh? I'm sure Jon's respect was far from his mind. . .and it was starting to disappear from my mind, too. I couldn't believe the thoughts running through my head.

My love for Jon was stronger than the Great Wall of China, but my lust for Marc was building into something new and unique, like the pyramids of Egypt — strong and speechless. I wrote him before he could say anything else.

> Natalie: *Marc, yes I am attracted to you, but I can't do anything about it. I'm with Jon. No matter how much my body groans to have you next to it, I can't act on it. I just can't.*

I waited on a response back but he didn't respond. I needed him to respond. Just bow out gracefully and we can move on to my computer issues; anything to keep my mind and body from having a war. Just a simple, "Ok, I'll leave you alone." Anything.

But there was no response. Then I heard his voice from around the corner.

"I can," he said.

He stalked from around the wall to see me sitting there nervous; extremely nervous over what was going to happen through this unfair proposition.

"You can what?" I responded back.

"I can act on it."

He walked around my desk as I stood up in complete shock. He was in front of me, confronting the passion and lust that was lying between my legs.

"Marc…"

But before I could say another word, his lips enveloped mine. He kissed me soft at first, until he felt my body give in and then he trapped me with his tongue in my mouth. His hands shifted from rubbing my waist and back to caressing the top of my ass. The voice inside of my head told me to push him away and walk out the office, but my body just wouldn't let me. We broke from each other and I was stuck in a glare-off with him.

We looked into each other eyes, much like we had before when I saw the glimmer, but this time there was a fire about to be unleashed.

He took in my lips again, this time more forcefully backing me into my table. He lightly lifted me up and sat me on the table without even breaking our embrace. My fingers rolled over each chiseled muscle in his back, feeling each flex with each flick of his tongue with mine. His hand moved from my ass to the front of my hoodie.

He began to unzip it, revealing my semi-naked chest. As fast as he shifted to my hoodie, he pulled off my gauchos even quicker, leaving me with just my black-lace bra and purple-satin thong.

He released his kiss and took a step back, as if he wanted to take a mental picture of the trail he was about to blaze on my body. He slowly took off his shirt to unmask his smooth, immaculately-sculpted chest. For a moment, I wondered if he was a personal trainer, or just my very own personal demi-god. My heart started racing, anticipating touching his wonderfully structured chest all the way down to his awaiting v-zone. His sweatpants soon fell down revealing his monstrous, protruding mass just screaming to be released.

"Does he take his time with you?" He whispered to me.

He approached me and put his lips on my neck to suck it as if he had just tasted a strawberry for the first time.

He felt so good!

His hands found my hard nipples with additional goose bumps. He circled my left nipple then took no time putting the other in his mouth. I moaned from the warmth of his mouth as his tongue did the same flicker on my nipple that it had in my mouth.

"Does he make sure you get what you need?"

He moved his mouth from my left breast to the right breast and back again.

He introduced me to his multitasking skills by adding in his hand, moving it slowly down to caress my cove. I felt his mass rub against my leg and grabbed it, taking my time stroking slowly up and down – up and down. He slid my thong to the side, gently teasing my wetness with his mass. Our wet, naked parts were meeting for the first time and it felt amazing. I grabbed his mass a little tighter and he guided first one and then two fingers in and out of me, while not missing a beat with his tongue on my nipples.

"Does he take time to taste you?"

His hand soon traded places with his month. He enveloped all of my pussy in his month now using his tongue like his fingers. I grab his head and pulled it close.

"Hold on." He made sure my hands were trapped on his head while he seemed to enjoy being trapped in my paradise.

My hips began to gyrate as we created our own rhythm mixing his licks, my moans and the table hitting the wall. He continued until I came loud enough that I was sure that if anyone else was in the building, no matter what floor, they would have heard me.

Marc stood up in front of my now completely-naked body with his dick at full mass, ready to dive in, but he didn't at that moment.

"My turn."

He grabbed my hand and led me to his office. He had one of the largest windows in the office and in front of it he placed his desk — the spot he had chosen to devour me. In one sweep, he pushed documents to the floor and knocked figures and paper weights across the room, preparing my new resting spot. He lifted me up and placed me firmly on the desk, showing me that it was time for round two. Simultaneously, he kissed and entered me, gently.

The pressure from his mass stretched out my cove in new ways. Pain was definitely pleasure. He leaned me back on the desk and lifted one leg and then the other over his shoulders, never leaving the depths of my passion.

I put my head back and yelled out in ecstasy as I was close to coming all over his desk. He now glistened with sweat beads that glowed in the afternoon sunlight.

His motion in and out of me was effortless and passionate with each stroke. Our bodies tensed up, preparing for our final climax. The release of our juices felt as if we had both taken our first breath together. Marc collapsed on top of my body, totally exhausted from our escapade. I closed my eyes, as he rested on my chest and thought about how great it was that I had locked the door after we came in.

Then I heard the phone ringing in the distance. It was Jon's ring. The satisfaction from the moment vanished and I was filled with guilt.

How could I have forgotten about my man? How could my body put my mind in such a disastrous situation? I could still feel the heat radiating off of Marc's body, but all I could think about was;

What about my Jon?

GROW UP

I'm scared to love him,

So, I'll just lust for his presence.

He's not like my man,

Only focused on what's evident.

I'm scared to lose him,

So, I'll give into his decadence.

I can't lose this new feeling,

This new sexual precedent.

I'm scared I'll need him,

Because my body calls to this new man.

Once the other finds out,

There's no way love will be able to stand.

But maybe I'm just too weak,

To walk in these new, unknown shoes.

Maybe love can conquer all,

And I just need to grow up and choose.

THE ROBINSONS'

I NEEDED A WEEKEND away to relax. I never took vacations because I had never had the time. My work was my air — only allowing me to inhale issues and exhale solutions. The running joke was that I, Nia Simone, was more than married to my work. I was having a threesome with my work and parking spot. It's fine though. I went to school to do this. My mom told me to get focused and be better than the rest and I am. So, I'm fine with the jokes since I'm the one watching from above. But I had to get real with myself — I needed a break.

"Bitch, you don't need a break you need a *fuck*!"

Talking to Amanda was so exhausting, but only because she said what I was really thinking even when I didn't want to think it.

"Shut up!" was the best response that I could give her.

"Yeah, you can deny it, but when was the last time you let someone bend yo' ass over and put you to sleep?"

The problem was that I couldn't deny my want for some intimacy. It had been years (yes, years) at least five, since I'd felt the warmth of a man between my legs. My career satisfied my desire for success, but not my desire for lust.

"You know what you need?"
I was scared to ask, "what?" but I knew she wouldn't let me hang for too long.

"You need a weekend getaway. Just a quick trip to relax your mind and body."

"Maybe more of my mind than my body. . ."

"Yeah, whatever. You need a break. Why don't you go to an island?"

"An island?"

"Yeah! Go get your groove back."

"I'm twenty-seven, not forty-something. Try again."

We both laughed.

"Ok you're right. How about MIA."

"Miami?? Yeah, I don't think that's a good idea. Too many whackos there."

"Yeah there are, but there are also some fine-ass men too."

"Married, I bet."

I rolled my eyes, because I've heard of the so-called bachelor scene. It's those men who take off their rings who are all of a sudden, "available".

"Look, you need a break. You're not looking for relationship, you're not looking for love *per se*, you're looking for a break. A release. Some fun shit!"

I hated when she was right. I just needed to get away and not think about anything — just be in the moment.

"Alright, you've sold me. Miami it is!"

Amanda ran over and gave me a hug. Her joy for my trip was weird, but understandable. She wanted me to live my life and she felt like I was missing out on so much just going from work to home.

I planned my trip for the upcoming weekend. Another perk about working hard; it was easy for me to play hard. I saved all the time, so a quick, an expensive trip to MIA was nothing for me.

Before I knew it, Friday was here and I was walking through the airport. It was quick and easy, which almost made it feel like it was a sign. It took three hours, but an enjoyable three hours in first-class taking care of last-minute business items. Even on vacay I had work on my mind. Go figure.

"Hi, Ma'am, would you like something to drink or a snack?" The stewardess asked me.

"Sure. . .I'll have some water," I told her and then she rolled her eyes.

Did she just call me soft, or was that just in my mind?

"Excuse me, Ma'am. . ."

"Yes?" The redhead stewardess turned back to me.

"I'll actually have a shot. . .a shot of Patron. Do you have that?"

"Why, yes, we do!" Her attitude immediately changed. I couldn't help but be proud of myself. A shot to get the trip started.

"Here you go."

"Thanks." I nodded at her and gave her a tip, then slipped the top off and downed the shot.

Immediately a shiver went down my back. *Shit* I thought to myself. *Maybe I should have done a practice run before the trip.*

It was too late. I let the heat subside in my throat and then calm down through my chest.

"Good choice," this woman next to me whispered.

I turned to acknowledge her comment when I notice her radiant beauty. Now, I'm not into women, but this woman was gorgeous. Her dark hair complimented her greenish-brown eyes and pale pink lips. Her skin was flawless with only a few freckles on her checks. And her smile was so white and refreshing, I couldn't help but smile back.

"Yeah, I thought it was a good choice. . .at least before I took it."

She chuckled and even her laugh was soft and calming. Then I started feeling weird about noticing her qualities, so I slowly turned back to my purse to find my ear buds.

"Are you staying in Miami, or will this be a layover for you?" She asked.

"I'm staying in Miami." I responded, as I continued to search for my earphones. I finally found them at the very bottom, of course.

"I hope I'm not bothering you," she continued, "But, this will be me and my husband's first trip to Miami and we're pretty excited about it. Do you know the area?"

I looked back over at her and then noticed her husband leaning up from his seat. Were they real-life Ken and Barbie dolls? His light eyes, along with his brown mustache and goatee combo, made his lips look perfect — perfectly soft and perfectly ready. Ready for what, I had no clue, but they were ready for something fun.

"Hi," he waved at me showing a glimpse of his muscular bicep and sparkling wedding ring.

"Hi," I waved back and I decided to answer her question, trying my best to keep crazy thoughts out of my head.

"To be honest, this is my first time, too. I'm just going for a break so I'm going to go wherever the breeze may take me."

She shook her head in agreement.

"Well, this will be an adventure for us all. By the way, my name is Monroe Robinson and my husband's name is Andrew."

"It's nice to meet you both."

I put my hand out to shake hers and she gladly accepted.

We spent the rest of time just talking about our lives. Similar to me, she was the Director of Communications at a Fortune 500 company and he was CIO of an IT company. The Robinsons reveled in traveling around the US and a little internationally, owning a home in Martha's Vineyard, Paris and Hawaii. I envied their success, but it also gave me more drive to get where I was trying to go. She was the youngest of four and he was the only child. Both were passionate about making the most of their individual and married life. She dropped, "you only live once," at least four times throughout our conversation.

Normally, I dreaded airplane talk. But this conversation kept me engaged. I wanted to know more about the million-dollar life, even if they wouldn't admit that was where they'd come from. Monroe was so well-cultured, having traveled the world and even taking a year off to donate her time and money to an Afghan orphanage. I made it past her evident, undeniably-attractive physicality to discover a new mental attraction to her.

Before I knew it, the flight was descending and it was time to strap back in for our exit.

"Alright, Ladies and Gentleman, we are descending into Miami. There is a little turbulence, but we will be on the ground before you know it. Thank you so much for traveling with us."

With my seat belt on, tray table up and seat back forward, I prepared for the beginning of a much-needed vacation. The turbulence was strong. We hit one good gust and Monroe grabbed my hand. I looked over at her clinching her teeth and holding her breath. I turned and moved closer to her ear.

"It's ok. It will be over soon," I whispered to her.

She turned back to me and opened her eyes. I saw her take a breath and then smile.

"Thank you," she whispered back.

And then, she gave me a kiss on the cheek.

I quickly smiled back and turned to the others on the plane to see if they saw anything. This woman was more than affectionate: she was comfortable.

The trip from the airport to Ocean Bed Hotel was quicker than I thought it would have been. It must have been because my mind focused on the beach. . .yeah, I think that was it. The hotel was lavish. There was an indoor/outdoor pool on two floors and a free happy hour for guests from 7-9pm.

Time flew by so fast that the happy hour was in effect before I had even started changing my clothes.

I guess I lost track of time as I walked up and down South Beach. Between the big, frozen drinks to the scandalously-dressed women and shirtless men, I felt like I was in another world; a world where everyone was comfortable in their own skin. It didn't matter if you were black, white, fat, skinny, tall, short, natural or silicon-filled; you were just excited to be there and show off what you were. I mean, there was someone with nothing on but a thong and strings covering their nipples. If they were comfortable, who was I to judge?

I quickly changed into my tropical print mini-dress with a pair of comfy, but tall, stilettos and headed down to the bar. By now it was packed. I pushed my way to the bar and gestured to the bartender.

"Can I help you?" The fine-ass Latin bartender asked.

"Why, yes! I'll take Patron on the rocks with a splash of lime."

"Sure, and by the way, my name is Romel," he responded.

As I waited on my drink, I took in the people around me — mostly young, late 20s men and women who were super-attractive. I didn't know if I'd just come on the right weekend or what, but everyone in Miami just seemed so beautiful.

The bartender finally came back with my drink. I took a sip, gave him the "good job" nod and left his tip. Then I remembered I had forgotten to ask him a question.

"Hey, Romel!" I yelled down the bar, trying to catch him before he went to his next patron.

He swiftly turned back. "Yes, Ma'am?"

"What's going on tonight? Like where does everyone go?"

"It depends. Are you into house music or hip-hop?"

I really felt I could do anything, but I was in the mood for some hip-hop and told him so. He gave me a quick run-down of the nearby clubs, but told me that his favorite Friday night spot was a club called YOLO up on Collins Avenue.

"Sounds cool. I'm game."

"When I get off at 10pm I'm going to head up there. Will I see you?"

He was young and gorgeous, so of course I answered, "You just might."

My glass of Patron and I took a seat next to the pool. Even with all the people, lights and music blasting from cruising cars, I found peace in being in a different place outside work. It was refreshing. It was new. Hell, it was sexy!

Everything seemed so easy and smooth. I plotted a way to extend my vacation, but soon realized I had WAY too many projects on hold in my absence. Maybe next time, I chuckled to myself.

Before I knew it, it was 9:30pm and I was definitely starting to feel my drink.

I left the empty glass on the table and passed the bar with a "see you later" wave to Romel. I was off to indulge in the city. I passed couples fawning over each other, bachelor parties yelling for my attention and even a mature couple just enjoying the live, colorful entertainment. Soon I was at Story, but the line was almost around the block. I walked to the front of the line. I checked my hair and adjusted my dress, focused on getting the bouncer's attention.

"Excuse me." I yelled to the bald, fit one. To my surprise he heard me and headed my way.

"How can I help you?"

"How much does it cost to get in through this line?"

"$40." he said, looking back to check his post.

"I can give you a $100 if you can let me in now. I'm by myself." I gave him the sultry eyes.

"I don't know, Ma'am."

"Plllleaaasee!" I begged him with a winning smile.

He took the velvet rope down and I immediately went in my purse for the cash. I made my exchange and he personally walked me to the door.

~ 91 ~

"Thank you!"

"Have a great time." I could barely hear all his words as the door opened.

The music was loud with T-Pain's *I'm in Love with a Stripper* blasting in the background. The place was huge.

There were people everywhere already and VIP tables filling up. I made my way to the nearest bar to request a Tequila Sunrise.

With my new drink in hand, I decided to just do a couple of rounds. The main floor was massive with the DJ booth located on the stage, where go-go dancers danced in cages on each side. The strobing lights were methodic and took the atmosphere to another level.

There was smoke in the air – blunts, blacks and hookahs. . .Oh My.

I finished my stroll on the other side and decided to do as much people-watching as I could. Then I felt a tap on my shoulder.

"Hey!"

I was greeted with a hug from Monroe. She was dressed in a tight, low-V front dress with platform shoes to match. Andrew followed up her hug with one of his own. He was also dressed in black – black button-down and black shorts with loafers.

"Hi! What are you guys doing here?"

"What?"

I had forgotten for a second that we were in a club. I cleared my throat and took my voice up a notch.

"What are you guys doing here?" I yelled back at them.

Monroe grabbed my hand and pulled me past the bar to a section where the music was a little lower.

"So much better. Now...what were you saying?"

"I was just wondering what you guys were doing here?"

"Trying to get in some trouble."

We both laughed and she continued, "We just wanted to get out. Enjoy the city a little. Are you here alone?"

"Yeah. Solo-dolo." I responded.

As soon as the words left my lips I realized how lame I sounded. I mean really – who comes to Miami alone?

"That's interesting" she responded. "Well, feel free to hang out here with us. We got a section just for the two of us so I can sit down once these shoes start killing my feet."

"I totally understand! And thank you."

She grabbed my hand and replied, "No problem".

She locked eyes with me again, quietly creeping me out, but I kept my cool and just took a drink. The night went on and the club filled up.

We danced. We laughed. We drank. Soon Monroe was full and dancing with everyone, including other men and women, but always coming back to Andrew.

Andrew didn't seem bothered by her momentary lap dances on others. He just smiled and took a sip of his drink. It was weird, but at the same time attractive to see a man so confident and comfortable with his woman.

Men that I've seen in similar situations normally end up getting kicked out the club for trying to fight or just stood up for the night because another man just took his girl. But the Robinsons' relationship was different. It was honest and real; open but trusting. It was new to me.

The mood shifted and a slow song came on over the speakers.

I started swaying from side to side, letting the music take my mind to another place where I had my own Andrew; someone who wanted no one but me; someone who complemented me; from my career and personal endeavors to my sexual needs and yearning to be unconditionally loved.

In my daze I could feel a man's hands grab my waist, swaying to the beat with me, then pushing up against me, but still to the beat. I let my imagination run and indulged him by pushing my ass up against him. I could feel him getting longer and harder. I smiled to myself and laid my head back on his chest.

He gripped my hips harder, pulling them closer and tighter to his staff. It felt good and fit right into my fantasy.

I opened my eyes. It was Andrew. I immediately stopped and looked to see where Monroe was. She was on the dance floor dancing with a guy, but looking dead at us. I took two quick steps from him, totally embarrassed. Even more so, feeling disrespectful of the marriage I had just been admiring.

Monroe started walking toward me, as I was now standing back at the bar. I turned away trying to get the bartender's attention but also trying to separate myself from this, "hell, naw, bitch" moment I had created.

She tapped me on the shoulder. My first thought was to just ignore her, but then I thought it would be bad to let her get a cheap shot in on me from the back. I turned to her with my muscles tense like I was preparing for some sort of altercation. Again we were face to face. She leaned over to say something in my ear.

Before she could say something I started in. "Look I'm…"

"It's ok," she whispered.

I jerked back. "What is ok?" I responded.

"I'm totally comfortable with Andrew being with other women."

"Really?"

They must have been made for each other. It was the freaking weirdest relationship I had ever seen, but on the other hand it sort of made sense. They were two well-accomplished, attractive people who had a long-standing relationship and now a marriage. They were totally comfortable in their lives. A little dumbfounded at my new reflection, I tried to end the conversation the best I knew how to for this type of situation.

"Tonight, you need to fuck your man," I told her. I couldn't believe that was the next thing to fly out my mouth. It had to be the liquor.

She laughed so hard and long from my comment that I was now totally embarrassed and ready to exit the club. Then she finally came down from the laughter to respond.

"I know…I know. Would you like to also?"

I didn't think I heard her right. I mean, we were in a club and it was really loud so there was no way she could have said what I thought she said.

"I'm sorry, what did you say?"

She laughed and threw her head back again as if she had never heard something so funny; even after my last dumb comment.

She stopped laughing. "I said, would you like to fuck him, too?"

I pulled back from her and as soon as I did she grabbed my hand once again. She pulled me back in again but so close that our cheeks almost touched.

Then she whispered, "Please…you're beautiful and we would like to invite you back to the room with us."

Now, I started laughing like she was Dave Chappelle, putting on a mini-stand up concert for me. Was she serious? How could she be? There's no way.

I whispered back to her, "You are so funny. You guys have a good night."

Before I could pull back to make my exit she grabbed my hand again, this time interlocking her fingers with mine. I immediately felt something I hadn't before; different and a little shocking.

"I'm not scared to beg," she told me. "You are what we need."

With her hand still attached to mine, I turned around to look at him. His eyes immediately locked with mine. He bit his lip at me as if he was imagining what he would do to me. I felt that feeling again, this time heating my body from my cove to my extremities.

Was this peer pressure from the situation that was circling my body? It couldn't be. I'm a power woman; no one makes me do anything I don't want to do, but then what was it I wanted to do?

I felt her begin to rub my back from lower to the nape of my neck. I closed my eyes, forgetting my surroundings for one second and then it hit me. I was desire. Underneath my confusion and even fear of a threesome situation, I desired these two unbelievably attractive people who happened to be husband and wife.

Could I actually do this? Was it just the alcohol talking? Probably not. My work-heavy, people-focused life was so exhausting. Maybe I could do this one thing for me. . .for my body. . .for my desire.

My eyes opened with him now taking a sip of his drink. I smiled and raised my favorite eyebrow. What the hell! I turned back to her.

"Okay," I whispered.

"What?" She apparently couldn't hear me but I knew she needed to listen closer before I chickened out.

"Okay. . .Let's do this."
It finally registered with her what I'd said—so much so that she kissed me on my cheek, which freaked me out a little. But the freaking out was just beginning.

"Let's go."

She stood up and turned to her friend to let her know of her exit, again not letting our interlocking hands depart from each other. She brought me over to her husband as if she was presenting me. He grabbed my hips and pulled me in for a neck kiss. It was warm and soft almost like a "thank you" for my body.

Somehow, Andrew made it out of the club before me and Monroe, and already had the driver waiting. *Excited much*, I thought to myself. Andrew opened the door and we all hopped in the black Suburban headed toward my hotel.

"What hotel are you guys staying at?"

Monroe responded, "The Ocean Bed."

Maybe I was starting to sober up but the thought of me walking to the Robinsons' room, in the same hotel where I'd just met a bunch of people freaked me out.

"Oh," was all that I could get out.

Andrew was sitting behind me and Monroe when he asked if we wanted something to drink. "No. I'm sure I've had enough," I chuckled.

"Yeah we all have, so that's why I was asking about water. I would hate for you to get sick and our night end early."

So that was his angle — trying to make sure I don't mess up the night with any drunken heaves. How selfish.

He got up from his seat and kneeled in front of me with a bottle of water.

"Here, take a sip for me."

He opened the bottle and put it up to my mouth. I took a small sip and then a large one, taking several big gulps with my eyes closed. A little spilled out on my last gulp, trickling down the front of my dress and into my lap. Andrew grabbed a napkin, wiped my mouth then my neck, and proceeded down the v-cut preview of my breast finally ending on my lap. He made sure not to be too rough, but sure enough to not miss a spot. I could feel my body starting to warm up.

"There you go," he smiled at me. "Please let me know if you need anything else. . .please."

I knew he was pleading for so much more.

We finally arrived at the hotel and quickly made a dash to the elevators. I was first to enter and they followed, standing on either side of me; the symbolic sandwich, making me wonder once again what I was getting myself into. Their room was on the tenth floor; the penthouse suite. I should have known. Unfortunately, the ride in the elevator seemed to take forever as people were continuously getting on and off. I started wondering again if this was another sign. Was God giving me more time to think this through or even walk away?

What am I doing? I thought to myself. Was I this desperate to just allow myself to be a sexual object for some rich, over-privileged and probably just sex-crazed people? Why couldn't I just find my own man and not a married one and not a woman?

Right as I was prepping myself to express my chicken-ness, I felt Monroe's hand interlock with mine. Her grip was tight but for some weird reason, calming. Then as if he, too, felt my apprehensions, Andrew grabbed my other hand to pull it to his mouth for a kiss. I turned to look at him and our eyes met. He didn't smile or smirk at me, he just looked into me as if he saw something he had never seen before. And then the elevator opened.

With my hand still interlocked with hers, Monroe guided me into a chic loft- like penthouse with nothing but windows and artwork everywhere. The black and white decor created a beautiful backdrop for the glassworks and incredibly large masterpieces.

"This is beautiful!" I told them.

"Not as beautiful as you," Andrew responded.

As cliché as it was, it made me respond but then I remembered that his wife was also in the room. I turned to her and saw nothing but a smile on her face. This shit couldn't get any weirder.

"Would you like anything to drink?" She asked.

"A glass of wine, please."

She laughed, but shook her head in agreement. I think she could see right through my calm demeanor, right down to the confusion and even the apprehension.

"Excuse me, Ladies. I'll be right back."

We nodded in unison. She asked me what type of wine I wanted and I responded with, "anything," which made us both laugh.

As she was getting the glasses and wine together, we made more small talk about my life and where I really wanted to go. I told her I had no real clue, other than being my own boss at some point. She continued with question after question, asking me about my family and did I want to start my own. It was as if she was truly into who I was and not what I was doing there.

I began to drop my guard more, even telling her about my reason for coming to Miami and how Amanda had jokingly labelled me as a "Stella" who needed her groove back. I soon lost myself in our conversation, taking a sip here and there but more focused on getting to know her and letting her get to know me. We even touched on how many sex partners we had had to date. I told her I could count them on one hand and she told me she could, too. . .but it was really just one finger. Andrew was her first and only. She said she had never yearned for another man or person; that is until she met me.

"And speaking of that. . ." I lead in, "why did you ask me to join. . .I mean. . .why now and why me?"

"We have always been honest to each other, Drew and I. And as much as we love being with each other, it gets stale from time to time."

"Oh, so I'm here to spice up the relationship?"

"No, not really. When we met on the plane, you were just interesting. And for the first time, I seemed to have an attraction to another woman and not just in a friendly way. It was more than that. It was sexual wrapped in mysterious mixed with comfortable. I know that doesn't make sense, but I just felt something different with you. I wanted you in some way."

"So did you and Drew, if I can call him that, talk about me?"

"Sure. To be honest, I couldn't stop talking about you. He was the one to point out that I really liked you and he admitted that you were gorgeous, so that probably helped."

I blushed and tried to continue figuring out why we were in the place we were.

"So, then what? You guys were like, 'Then let's get her'?"

"NO." She abruptly shook her head. "Definitely not. We aren't predators."

"I'm sorry. I didn't mean it like that. I just want to know how we got to this point. You know. . .a threesome."

She came from the kitchen and sat next to me on a bar stool.

"When we saw you at the club, I was so excited to see you. I immediately wanted to come over and give you a hug and kiss like I missed you. Which to be honest, felt weird as shit and actually made me wonder what the fuck was going on with me."

Hearing her talk about these feelings made me realize that they were mutual; but why?

She continued, "Drew noticed you too and even pointed you out to me, so I could go over and talk to you. I told him that was a dumbass idea and what was I going to say. That's when he took me over to the bathroom and told me his thoughts.

He said, 'Roe, I know things have been ok with us and maybe that is why you have these new feelings, but in all honesty I can't deny that I have an attraction to her too. So how about tonight we stop trying to think things through and let things happen? I'm not going to love you any less. I just want you to be happy.' So I told him that I wanted you and he agreed that he wanted you too."

What an honest, but still weird conversation to have, but I guess there is no good way to talk about liking another woman with your husband. . .I guess.

"So that's why when we came back, he grabbed you. He wanted to feel you and I actually liked watching you two. I liked watching you."

I blushed more and looked down at my glass. It was different hearing another woman say these things about me; especially this beautiful, successful woman. But, the facts were that I felt the same way about her. I was intrigued by her too. I wanted to be close to her. I wanted to explore these feelings, these same feelings she was having.

Monroe took both of my hands in with hers, making me face these feelings head-on.

"Can I kiss you. . .please?" She begged.

I didn't respond verbally. I allowed myself to release and leaned in to kiss her. First a peck. Then a longer kiss. Before I knew it, her tongue was in my mouth and mine in hers. I began to rub her shoulders and then down her arms.

Then, she took my hands and placed them on her face. She leaned back away from me and just looked into my eyes.
It was the same desired look that Drew had given me on the elevator.

And then it began.

She moved my hair from my neck and began kissing it. It felt so good. Her kisses were soft and perfect. She took her time going from one side of the neck to the other. I coached her by pulling her closer and rubbing up and down her back, just stopping at the top of her buttocks. I could feel her body arching into mine.

As her kissing started to move down into my chest, I felt a second set of hands rub my shoulders. Drew was back and I could feel his bare chest on my back. Then, his kisses started around my neck and down my back. He untied my halter and let if fall slowly off my shoulders, revealing my naked breasts.

Monroe took my left breast into her mouth, as if she knew exactly what I wanted and I did not fight it. I stared to unfasten her dress. Then, I unzipped it. She stood up and I watched it fall off her body, revealing every ounce of her greatness. Her body was exceptional. Her skin was lightly-tanned and a rose tattoo was etched on her inner left thigh. She grabbed my hands and stood me up.

Drew walked over to me and proceeded to pull my dress down from around my waist and then completely off me. I thought I was going to feel uneasy and nervous about standing nude in front of these two, but I wasn't. I was comfortable and ready. With their hands now back entangled with mine, I followed Drew to the bed.

He turned back around to me and kissed me deep. I felt his hands move warmly over my bottom, grabbing and rubbing each part of my skin. Then, I looked over and saw Monroe now lying on the bed, watching and waiting for our next moves. I moved my hands to his belt and completely removed it.

I unbuttoned and unzipped his slacks, releasing his monster. I had come in with no expectations and was more than pleased to see him hanging down to his mid-thigh.

I never thought he would be so well-endowed. Now, I get why he was her only. I locked eyes with him as I lowered myself past his defined abs, even lower past his masterful V and then to his shaft. I had never been so excited to see how deep I could really take him. My mouth was ready, wet for his flavor. I took him in my mouth slowly at first and a little faster.

I could see Monroe now coming toward me. She got behind me and held back my hair from my face. She wanted to watch as much as he did. I hummed from his deliciousness and she showed her enjoyment by kissing my back and neck. She then moved her hand down in between my crouched legs.

My cove was so warm and wet that her first touch almost immediately put me over. I responded by throwing my head back and letting out a moan.

I went back to him, using the pleasure she was giving me on him. His thickness was getting stronger and longer. I could feel he was getting close. He quickly pulled me back up and kissed me deeper again, but then ended the kiss by throwing me on the bed. I chuckled and watched Monroe climb slowly on top of me. She took her hands and used them to memorize my curves. She made a pit-stop at my cove to give it a kiss and two licks. I wanted more, but she moved up my stomach and back to my breasts. The pleasure was unbelievable.

I could feel us touching. Her wetness complimented mine. Our bodies rubbed together creating heat between us. She came up for a kiss and then I felt Drew kissing us between our legs. I felt his tongue dart inside of me and sucking my clit and then I felt his chin moving up and down, now attaching to Monroe's cove. Her pleasure was as pleasing as my own. I grabbed her ass as he went back to me, and I allowed my fingers to dip in and out of her. She loved it.

"More," she pleaded to us both.

He stepped over the dresser to grab a condom and quickly put it on. Then he slipped deep inside me. Each thrust rocked all of our bodies. She kissed me continuously and I didn't know how much longer I could hold on. Then he jumped out of me and dipped into her. Her moans were loud and pleasing.

I returned the kisses back to her and she held me tighter. Then she grabbed my hands and pushed my arms above my head.

Drew took control, staring right at me. "I want you to come for me, please."

He plunged back into me and while holding on to her hips, he took me deep; each stroke stronger than the last; each stroke focused on pushing me to the edge. I slipped my fingers back inside of her. I wanted her to come with me. Our bodies moved together in an erotic rhythm. I moaned and she cooed. He moaned and then I cooed. Soon, I couldn't hold it anymore.

"More!" I told them and he sped up while I did the same with my fingers. Then, I felt the release of my juices spill on top of him, clenching tight around him while her cove did the same as she let out a strong moan on my neck. He matched her moan with his own grunt, falling over her.

Monroe rolled over and spooned my left side. Then Drew came and laid on my right side, placing his arm around me, pulling me close but also grabbing Monroe's waist. We all lay in the bed and just allowed the moment to sink in. I had never felt so comfortable with two people more than I felt at that moment. I felt their warm embraces as if it was all just one huge hug.

I was the Robinsons' and they were mine.

ABOUT THE AUTHOR

Since an early age, DNC has been writing about life's adventures, love stories and the challenges women face. After rebounding from the devastating sudden loss of her mother, she turned to her writing as a therapeutic outlet. This time, revealing a more personal imagination — her inner sexual imagination.

DNC currently resides in Atlanta, GA enjoying the family life as a wife and mother of three, while simultaneously pursuing her passion in writing and marketing – pushing to deliver on her most poetic dreams.

As the precursor to a series of books, *Untraditional* allows readers to safely indulge in a world of lust where they can step out of the norm and allow the mind to wonder down paths of pleasurable unsurety.

www.ingramcontent.com/pod-product-compliance
Lightning Source LLC
Chambersburg PA
CBHW021120130626
46554CB00002B/791